GOLDY,
SUPERHAMSTER

BOOKS
FOR
BOYS

Collect them all!
Why not try these other **Books for Boys**:

GOLDY, SUPERHAMSTER

Books for Boys

IAN WHYBROW
ILLUSTRATED BY MARK BEECH

Hodder
Children's
Books

A division of Hachette Children's Books

My New Beginning

My first text message to the boy read:

That was before I learned about commas or full stops or capital letters.

5

Still, it wasn't bad, was it? Not for a hamster.

Allow me to introduce myself. My name is Goldy. I am 13 centimetres long. I have a band of white round my middle but I am mostly golden. My tail is rather short but Ludo says I have ears like tulips and a beautiful nose. He also says I am a genius.

I was born in a laboratory with three brothers and four sisters. They were taken away before I got to know them and then I was given a cage to myself, one of a long row. Professor Sedley was my friend. He kept my cage clean, changed my straw and filled my water bottle. He was especially keen to know how different kinds of food changed my behaviour, so I had plenty to eat.

He would sit and study me for hours. He watched me run on my whizz-wheel. He was interested in the way I made my nest with different materials. He gave me seeds and vegetables and watched. I carried on as before. He tried me on insects. I liked them, but didn't do anything unusual. He watched what I did after eating dried cat food. There was no difference.

Finally he made the Special

Mixture for me. I'm not sure what was in it. At first I didn't like the taste of it or the smell of oily fish. But I got used to it and then I grew to love it. I filled my cheek pouches to bursting and stuffed so much of it into my nest that there was hardly room for me. And wow! It changed me!

The Special Mixture made me feel strong and full of energy. More than that, it made me feel brainy. I started thinking and having clever  ideas about all sorts of things. I began to whizz faster and faster on my wheel and try

out things with
my toys. Soon I
found that I could
do backward flips
and balance a
cotton reel on my nose
for ages. That got Professor Sedley
very excited. He ran to bring other
white-coats to see me. A flock of
them arrived holding shiny pads. I
didn't know then what these pads
were but I thought: "Woah! Careful,
Goldy! Think! If you show these
humans how clever you are, you
could be in this cage for the rest of
your life!"

You see, I had already decided I
would like to leave my cage and
explore the Outside.

So when the white-coats crowded round my cage, I didn't do anything clever. I did a bit of climbing, a bit of wheel-work, I ate, I drank and I tidied my nest. I just did normal hamster things.

Nothing special.

Building Up My Brainpower

My plan worked. The white-coats were disappointed and went away. Excellent! Now I was able to begin my close study of Professor Sedley.

The main thing I noticed was that, like me, he had very regular habits. When I came out of my nest he would sit beside me with his shiny pad; when I went to bed, he went away.

I studied the way he tapped the

keys on his pad and I worked out that somehow he was storing my life in there in the same way as I stored food in my nest. I could also see that when he lifted the pad up, he could capture moving pictures of me. I knew he was trying to record me doing something extraordinary but I wouldn't let him. For most of the time I did nothing except bustle about and chew things. Still, I knew I had to keep him interested for a while, so sometimes, when his fingers were busily tapping away on the pad, I would do something to amaze him.

For example I might make a pyramid out of sunflower seeds. Again, I might spit nuts into the air

one at a time and
bicycle-kick them
into my food
tray. That got
his attention!
He made a
little sound, his eyes grew very big
and he quickly pressed the pad to
his face. By then I was in my nest.

"Ha ha!" I said to myself. "Too
slow, Professor!"

Of course, he wasn't stupid.
When he saw me spinning round
on my head like a break-dancer he
moved his arm very, very slowly
and tried to capture some pictures
of me in a sneaky way. Zip! Back in
my nest I popped! He missed me
again.

When he tried to outsmart me by changing my food, I refused to do anything. I pretended I was ill and lay in the corner of the cage, panting and twitching. After that, he only ever fed me on Special Mixture.

Gradually Professor Sedley must have decided that his Special Mixture was no better than regular hamster-food at making me clever.

At last he lost interest in me and started studying the animals in the cages next to mine. Now that I had been left in peace, I could work on my plan to escape. It didn't take me long to work out how to open my door.

I waited until there were no white-coats about, slipped the catch and set off to explore the laboratory.

I was dying to find out how the shiny pads worked, and there were plenty of them lying about for me to get my paws on. The first time I used one I was dreadfully nervous. The pad I was examining suddenly went PING! It gave me such a fright that I scuttled back to my cage and hid in my nest, all-of-a-tremble.

Still, I had had my first smell of the Outside. That gave me the courage I needed to leave my safe little home, and explore new places. Every time I went out, I rubbed my nose against the scent-gland I have on my hips and left my mark somewhere in the laboratory. That way I made a detailed smell-map of it and came to know exactly which path to follow to reach where I wanted to be. Also, I practised harder and harder at using a pad. The effort of dancing on the keys in the right order gave me a headache but I kept at it and taught myself typing and texting.

Then came THE SHOCK!

One day, without warning, Professor Sedley threw a cloth over my cage, picked it up and carried me on a long bumpy journey. All those loud noises! All those strange new smells! It was terrifying but also thrilling.

When the cloth came off, I found myself blinded by daylight. This was new to me, so I tried to hide in my

nest. A warm hand reached into my cage and stopped me. I was lifted up and found myself gazing into the face of a small human. He was not a white-coat. He had straight teeth and a round face with dark fur coming down straight above his round, grey eyes. He carried some words on his chest.

I felt his breath on me, warm
and welcoming, and at once I knew
I had found a friend.

My New Home

Professor Sedley had a mate called Ma-mee. Sometimes they called my friend Boy or Sun or Sunshine, and sometimes, Ludo. I liked the name Ludo best.

It didn't take long to find out that Ludo and I had a great deal in common. To Professor Sedley and Ma-mee, Ludo was not just an infant. He was their pet, just as I was his. Our job was to please our owners and make them feel good.

Ludo and I both lived in a cage, though his was much bigger. We were both well fed and given things to do for exercise. I had my plastic tunnels, my cotton reels and my whizz-wheel; Ludo had only a strange machine called a violin that he tucked under his chin – and that was about all he had to keep him busy.

 Every morning, Professor Sedley would leave to go to the laboratory. Then Ma-mee would sit at her piano and watch Ludo closely, tapping her foot. Before I understood

what it was, I thought that the piano was a huge black beastie with terrible teeth. She would make it roar and thunder while Ludo scraped his machine with a stick and waggled his body about at the same time.

Sometimes Ludo's machine made a beautiful noise like hundreds of whizz-wheels squeaking different notes. Sometimes Ludo could make the machine patter like rain or whistle like a bird.

Sometimes it would laugh, but mostly it cried.

When Professor Sedley came home, he would sit down at a table with Ma-mee and Ludo and have a fight about food. Ludo would only ever eat a little of what was on his dish, then he would make some angry sounds and push it away. I soon came to understand what the sounds were. They were words, and they meant: "Why can't I have a hamburger sometimes, like normal, ordinary children?"

Professor Sedley's answer was: "Because you are NOT normal or ordinary. You have a first-rate brain. If you stay home and do what Ma-mee and I tell you, you will soon be able to play the violin better than any other child in the world. It is my job to study how food helps the brain, and Ma-mee's job to make sure you do your violin practice. And as I keep telling you, hamburgers are second-rate food for second-rate children!"

What else did we have in common? Well, Ludo and I had no friends except each other. And though I didn't know it at first, we shared the same dream. We both wanted to be free to explore the

Outside. Luckily for us, we both happened to be geniuses.

Even after only a few days living with Ludo, I quickly

understood that when Ma-mee stamped her foot and folded her arms across her chest, she was angry. I also learned that slamming a door can mean "No." It can also mean, "Leave me alone."

Every new day, the noises Ludo made on his machine sounded more and more horrible. Ma-mee made him keep scraping. Over and over.

Suddenly Ludo screamed. He threw down his machine and broke his stick.

Ma-mee sent him to his nest. He cried and cried. I knew it was time for me to send him a message to remind him that he wasn't alone.

There was a problem, though.

The cat.

A Near Miss

On my very first day in my new home, the cat leapt up and clicked his terrible claws along the bars of my cage! I  can't tell you what a shock it was to see savage teeth up close! When he hissed and

26

yowled at me, I thought I would die.

Ludo came running to save me with a piercing yell – and got a nasty bite for his trouble. He soothed me and promised me that the cat would be kept out of the living room from then on. Nevertheless, it took quite a while for me to pluck up the courage to slip the catch and risk a run-about with no bars to keep me safe. Even in my dreams I could still smell the blood-lust of that furry monster.

Meanwhile, I had noted that humans have many pouches they call pockets, and that Professor Sedley always emptied his on the living-room table before he went off to his nest to sleep.

The most interesting items he set down – for, strangely, there was no sign of food – were the tissues and the phone. I considered taking a tissue to use as soft nesting material, but I did not want him to discover that I had been out of my cage. I concentrated instead on studying how the phone worked. Since it was smaller and lighter than the pads in the laboratory, I found I could manage it more easily – and after a few nights' practice I found I could, as humans say, surf the net.

I tried typing O-U-T-S-I-D-E and found myself looking at pictures of sports clothing. That made no sense to me. I had better luck with A-N-I-M-A-L-S. Until I learned the secrets of the internet I had no idea how many different kinds of us there are! I spent hours scrolling through to gaze at them.

I was so caught up in the wonder of it that I didn't hear the door to the living room swish open, or the pad of cat paws on the wooden floor.

It was only thanks to my keen sense of smell that I am alive to tell this tale. A whiff of fishy breath made me look up, and suddenly there they were –

two evil yellow-green eyes glowing in the dark!

How I found the strength to swing the phone and smack that cat on the nose, I shall never know. But that gave me the seconds I needed to set my paws flying over the keys.

Quick! Quick! Volume on. Hit the keys. Put in B-I-G D-O-G B-A-R-K. Paws over the ears, and hang on for dear life!

YERRRRR! WOOFF! RAFF! RAFF! YERRRRRRR-OOF!

Doors flew open all around. Lights flashed on … but not before I threw myself down in front of the open door of my case and did a brilliant impression of having a heart attack.

Needless to say, that was the last time I saw that particular cat.

Adventures with Ludo

Eventually I was ready to text Ludo.

I typed "hi ludo dont be sad im your friend". Then I hit "send" and waited.

Suddenly his round face appeared on the screen. I had just received my first video call! Ludo's eyes were wide and blinking with fear. "Wh-who is that?" he said.

"Eek," I answered.

He didn't seem to understand. I

could see him trembling. He looked as if he had just seen a lion! "Meek," I said. It was my  first word, or nearly. I tried again. "Meeeek. Goldeeeek," I squeaked.

"Wha ... what's happening?" he gasped, peering at the screen. "Who are you? Leave me alone or I'll call for help!"

"No! Pleee-d don't!" I begged. "Goldeek!"

"Goldy? Is that really you? It can't be!"

"Owk-dide!" I said. Wow, talking was hard!

"Goldy! Did you just speak to me?"

"Uh-huh," I said. "Dorry if I dartled you." I was really having trouble with S-sounds. "But I want to dee Owk-dide. Will you take me?"

"Outside?" he said. "You want me to take you outside? Now? Are you kidding? It's the middle of the night! Where are you now?"

I was trying to explain that I was standing on a stool in the living room, but at that moment it was too much for me. It didn't matter, though, because he ran in and grabbed me and rubbed me against his cheek. "Oh, Goldy!" he said, wetting me with his tears. "This is unbelievable! I hope it isn't a dream."

"I'm real," I said. "Feel my teeth." I nipped him gently so that he gasped and gave a little jump. "Can we hurry up?" I begged.

"Ouch!" he whispered with a little laugh. "OK! That's real enough. Wow! This is the most fantastic thing that ever happened to me! And you really want me to show you around outside? Well, come on! If we're going to do that, I need to get dressed!"

The Outside was big and chilly, but not very dark because of all the lights. Some of them were in the sky.

Ludo tucked me into the side of his woolly hat so I could see where we were going. Different scents were coming at me thick and fast, and now and then we would hear a roar from one of the huge creatures on wheels that lit up the wide strip in front of us with their bright eyes.

"Got to be careful crossing the road," Ludo muttered, half to me and half to himself. "Because of the cars."

Aha! Cars! So that's what they were! We reached the other side safely and came to a green place. Then I smelt more danger. "Look out, Ludo!" I warned.

He stopped and spun round so fast that he shook me out of his hat. He tried to catch me and break my fall, but still I hit the ground hard. "Run!" I squealed.

"What's the matter? Is it the cars?" cried Ludo, falling to his knees beside me.

"Enemy!" I squeaked and ran for my life along the gutter.

Unfortunately I didn't know about drains. In my panic I rushed blindly towards one. The second before I plunged to my death, Ludo dived full-length and scooped me up.

I thought my heart would burst with terror. He must have felt it flutter as he held me tight. "Be careful!" he whispered. "What was it that scared you?"

"B-behind you," I stammered.

"Wow! A fox!" he exclaimed, looking back over at his shoulder. His voice was full of wonder. "What a beauty!" he said. "I never thought I'd see one of those! And so tame! It's running through the park, look! Let's follow it and see where it goes!"

I knew now that I was safe with Ludo. It was lovely feeling the wind in my fur as he ran over the grass in that dark and deserted park. The fox was far too quick for him, of course, and Ludo was soon out of breath. He sat down, panting, but I soon smelled something else interesting. "Have you deen one of doze?" I asked, still having trouble saying "S".

Ludo couldn't see anything properly in the gloom. Suddenly he spotted what I was talking about. "You mean under the roundabout? Oh my goodness! A hedgehog! So cute!"

When the prickly little thing scuttled away and hid under a bush, Ludo decided to try out the roundabout. "Whoo!" he cried. I thought it was fun, too; a bit like my whizz-wheel. It made your head spin in a good way.

Ludo took me for a ride on everything: the slide, the swings, the seesaw, the climbing frame, the tightrope. I had never seen such happiness.

"We must come here again!" he panted. "But now, what I would really like is … a hamburger."

A Disappointment

By the time we got to the shopping centre, it was light and getting brighter. And there were more humans about. Some of them looked at Ludo with curiosity, reminding me of the way the white-coats looked at me in the laboratory. But most of them were in a hurry and moved on. A female stopped and said to Ludo, "You all right, sunny? You're up a bit early, ain't you?" I was surprised that she knew his name.

"I'm fine, thank you," said Ludo. "My Ma-mee has gone to the bathroom. Then we're going to have a hamburger."

"You'll have a bit of a wait, then," she said. "There's cleaning to do first!"

"I know," said Ludo. "Ma-mee's a cleaner." He hurried off towards the toilets and the woman went on her way.

"I didn't know Ma-mee was a cleaner," I said to Ludo. "I was telling a lie," he explained.

That made no sense to me at all.
"Come on, we have to make sure
that lady doesn't see me again," he
went on.

We found a little hiding-place
near Hamburger Heaven. A long
time passed and we could hear that
more and more humans were
beginning to move around us. Then
you could smell hamburgers cooking.
They reminded me of the cat-food
Professor Sedley used to give me,
quite nice. "Hmmm," said Ludo.
"I'm starving."

He started to pat his pockets,
forgetting I was in one hand.

"Hoy!" I squeaked.

"Sorry," he said. "Oh no! I've just
remembered. I haven't got any

money." He sighed. "So disappointing! We'll just have to go home."

As he walked away, still holding me in his hand, I felt his tears plop on me, hot, then cold. "Look, Ludo!" I said as we passed a shop I hadn't noticed before.

"A machine like yours!"

He managed to made his face happy for a moment. "You mean a violin? You're so clever, Goldy."

"Why did you break your stick?" I asked. "I

really loved to hear the noises you made."

45

"Thank you," he said. "Ma-mee thinks I'm getting worse and worse. I don't want to play if she hates what I do."

"Maybe you would play better on a different machine … I mean, violin," I suggested. "Give that one a try."

"We'll have to wait for the shopkeeper, then," murmured Ludo. So we sat in the doorway and waited.

Attracting Attention

"Are you sure you know what you're doing?" the shopkeeper asked Ludo. "These instruments cost a lot of money." He made lines come on the top of his face like Ma-mee when she was not pleased.

But when he heard the sounds Ludo made, he made a face that reminded me of Professor Sedley when he saw me doing a backflip! "Oh my giddy AUNT!" he cried.

"You are AMAZING! Keep going, keep playing!"

He flung open the door, ran outside and shouted: "Come in here! Listen to this kid! He's FANTASTIC! I've never heard anything like it in my life!"

I crouched on top of the piano where Ludo had placed me and made myself small. I was tempted to squeal and dance and do headspins – but this was Ludo's moment, not a time for me to be amazing.

And one by one and two by two,

humans came and filled the shop. When the shop was full, they packed into the doorway and before long a great crowd gathered and gazed in through the window. Ludo closed his eyes and the violin poured out a sound that trembled like the warm lights in the Outside sky.

A boy took off his cap, shouted "Wow-ee!" and began to move about in the crowd. Finally, he pushed inside the shop and stood in front of us. Ludo stopped playing and handed the violin back to its owner.

There was a noise like thunder! I was scared, but it was only the humans smacking their hands together!

"Here you go, mate," said the boy. "I collected this for you. I didn't

know what else to do. You're …
you're brilliant, you are!" And he
tipped a heap of coins on to the
piano stool. "I wish I could play the
violin like that," he said.

"Thank you. It takes practice, that's
all," said Ludo. His eyes were
shining with happiness.
"If you come to
my house I
can teach
you, if
you like."
"Really? That
would be so cool!" said the boy.

Then, in the blink of an eye,
Ludo's happy face was gone –
because when he looked up, there
stood Professor Sedley and Ma-mee.

I made myself even smaller, expecting angry shouting. But there was no need. For a minute I thought they were trying to squash the life out of him; but then, I had never seen them hug Ludo before.

"What are you doing here, Ludo?" asked Professor Sedley gently. "We thought we'd lost you!"

"We were so afraid!" wailed Ma-mee.

"I was too strict about your food," said Professor Sedley. "Forgive me."

"Please don't hate us. We just wanted you to be the best violin player in the world!" added Ma-mee. "I thought I had ruined everything by pushing you too hard – but just now you played like an angel!

How is it possible?"

"I don't hate you!" said Ludo. "I know you want the best for me. I needed a change, that was all."

I had just managed to edge to the corner of the piano lid, close enough to Ludo's ear to be able to whisper into it without anyone else noticing. "And a friend," I hissed. "Tell them you need a friend."

"And I needed a friend," he said, hastily taking me in his hand. "And now I've got two. Goldy and … what's your name?"

"Luke," said the boy with the cap.

"There you are. Now I've got two. Luke wants to learn the violin. I'm going to help him. And Goldy wants to get out more and explore."

Professor Sedley nodded. "I'm sure that can be arranged," he said. He turned to Luke and told him he was welcome to come to the flat any time.

"Is there anything else you'd like, dear?" said Ma-mee.

Ludo held me up to his cheek. "We just want a bit more room to run about, don't we, Goldy? And a bit more fun. And we'd like to do different things now and then. That would be lovely. Although I do like playing my violin well and being at home with you." He looked at the Professor and Ma-mee.

"Thank you, Ludo," they said.

"But I don't want to be treated like a pet any more," Ludo went on. "I want to do more things for myself. And to go out more and have fun."

"And have a hamburger," I whispered. I was curious to try a bite of one.

"Ahem," said Ludo, pointing to the pile of money. "And now for something COMPLETELY new. Now that I'm rich, I would like to treat everybody to a hamburger."

"An experiment!" cried Profesor Sedley. "What a good idea! There's nothing I like better than experiments!"

"Then why don't we all have a Knickerbocker Glory with extra fudge to follow?" said Ludo. He could see that enjoying yourself didn't have to end with a hamburger.

I am sorry to say that I don't  have the right words to describe the look on the faces of all the people who were listening. Let's just say that it was something like beautiful music.

A Promise

Maybe it was all the unusual excitement. Maybe it was the nibble of hamburger that Ludo slipped me while we were sitting at the table in Hamburger Heaven. Anyway, I couldn't stop myself. I had been quiet for too long. It was MY turn to show how amazing I could be.

I jumped on to the table and danced round the ketchup bottle on my hind legs. Then I stood on the

pepper pot whistling the tune of
Mozart's Eine Kleine Nachtmusik
while I juggled five sugar-lumps.

It was that special look on people's
faces that I was
after. I wanted
them to feel the
way Ludo's
playing made
people feel. And
then suddenly I
had a terrible
thought.

"Oh no!" I
squealed and hid under a pile of
napkins.

Luckily, Ludo's gentle hand came
after me. His finger stroked me
gently until I was calm again.

"What's up, Goldy?" he said, holding me gently. "You were fabulous."

Professor Sedley and Ma-mee were staring at me in wonder. "My goodness me!" breathed the Professor. "I never expected to be outsmarted by a hamster!"

"Well, my brain power has a lot to do with your Special Mixture, Professor," I told him.

"Thank you for telling me that, Goldy," he said. "That means a lot to a dry old stick like me."

I looked steadily at the three of them. "I want you to promise me something," I said. "All of you." I said the "s"-sounds perfectly. I was getting used to speaking.

"OK," everybody said. Their faces were serious, as if they promised hamsters things every day.

"Promise you won't tell anybody else about me," I said. "I want to be a secret."

"Why?" everybody asked.

"Well, because now I've seen the

Outside. And I've had fun, I really have. But I've discovered that hamsters don't like TOO much excitement. We're happy with a nice clean, warm home, plenty of food and exercise. Of course we like being picked up and stroked. And a run-about now and then is lovely. But mostly we like a quiet life."

"If that's what you really want ..." said Ludo.

"It really is," I said. So they all promised not to tell anybody else about me being a genius.

And so far, neither of us has had anything to complain about since.